College Road Trip

A novel based on the major motion picture

Adapted by Alice Alfonsi

Based on the screenplay by Emi Mochizuki & Carrie Evans
and Cinco Paul & Ken Daurio

Executive Producers Ann Marie Sanderlin, Raven-Symoné,
Michael Green, Anthony Katagas

Produced by Andrew Gunn

Directed by Roger Kumble

DISNEP PRESS

New York

Printed in the United States of America

First Edition
1 3 5 7 9 10 8 6 4 2

Library of Congress Catalog Card Number: 2007906284

ISBN-13: 978 1-4231-1280-8
ISBN-10: 1-4231-1280-6
For more Disney Press fun, visit www.disneybooks.com
Visit Disney.com/CollegeRoadTrip

CHAPTER ONE

The courtroom was packed. The trial was almost over. Only one more lawyer was waiting to be heard: seventeen-year-old Melanie Porter.

"Counsel for the defense will now make her closing statement," the judge announced.

This is it, Melanie thought.

Rising from her chair at the defense table, Melanie smoothed her skirt, nodded at the unsmiling judge, and then approached the jury box.

"Ladies and gentlemen of the jury," she began, "my client, Mr. Wolf, has been accused of horrible crimes. Destruction of property and attempted murder, but he is *innocent* of both."

Across the room, a boy leaped up from the prosecutor's table. "Objection!" he cried out. "Speculative!"

Uh-oh, Melanie thought, holding her breath.

The judge was quiet a moment. "I'll allow it," he finally said. Then he nodded at Melanie. "Proceed."

Melanie exhaled, her nerves growing shaky as her gaze swept over the "courtroom," which was really just a high school auditorium. Students, parents, and teachers packed the place, and a banner on the wall reminded her of what was on the line for her team: THE ILLINOIS MOCK TRIAL COUNTY FINALS.

I have *got* to win this case, Melanie thought, even if it is just a nursery crime!

Just then, she noticed her father making his way down the main aisle. He took a seat next to Melanie's mom and tossed her a big thumbs-up. Melanie's eyes brightened.

As the town's chief of police, James Porter was a local hero and a very busy man. Melanie hadn't expected him to show. But he had! With renewed confidence, she swiveled on her brand new shoes and faced the jury box.

"The state has not presented a single shred of conclusive evidence," Melanie argued, pacing back and forth. "Yes, one house was made of sticks and one of straw, but they were both built to code. As our expert witness has testified, there isn't a wolf on the face of the planet with enough lung power to topple a house of straw, let alone a house of sticks. In other words: a huff and a puff is not enough. A huff and a puff is not enough!"

"Objection!" the boy cried out again, his expression stern.

"To what?" the judge asked.

The boy scratched his head. "Rhyming?"

The judge rolled his eyes. "Overruled."

In the audience, Melanie's father elbowed the man sitting next to him. "That's my baby girl," he said with a proud grin.

"Ladies and gentlemen," Melanie concluded at the front of the packed room, "ultimately, what is this trial about? It's about someone wanting to get in, and being kept out. Guilty of property destruction? No! Guilty of attempted murder? Absolutely not! The only thing my client is guilty of is wanting to be let inside. To be accepted. Let's not slam the door in his face again. Let's find him just what he is—not guilty. Not by the hair . . . of his chinny chin chin!"

Less than an hour later, the student jurors finished their deliberations and filed back into the court-room. The judge turned to the head of the group.

"Madam Foreman, you've come to a decision?" he asked.

The young woman nodded. "Yes, Your Honor. We find the defendant *not* guilty."

Cheers and applause erupted in the auditorium. Melanie leaped up from the defense table and gave high fives to her teammates. Then she turned to her cute co-counsel.

"We did it, Hunter!" she cried.

The tall, handsome boy smiled adorably and opened his arms wide. Melanie's jaw dropped as she realized the hottest dude in school was stepping up to embrace her.

Bam!

In the blink of an eye, Hunter was knocked out of her field of vision. In his place was her father, grinning from ear to ear.

"Daddy's girl!" he cried, giving her a big bear hug.

Dad! Melanie thought as her father squeezed her tight. If there was a law against stealing the moment, you'd be on trial right now!

"You were just so amazing," Melanie's mom, Michelle, gushed a few minutes later.

The three of them were walking toward the high school's parking lot.

"That's what I'm talkin' about," her dad agreed. "You knocked that one out of the park! You do know he was guilty though, right?"

"Dad, this is about legal theory," Melanie pointed out. "Everything isn't just black and white. There are shades of gray."

Forever the hard-nosed cop, James Porter waved his hand. "Gray is just guilty with a good excuse."

Melanie stopped in her tracks, ready to prove her father's outrageous statement wrong, when her mom stepped between them. "O-kay," she said. "You both make interesting points, but the trial's over. My ruling is we go home and celebrate."

Melanie pursed her lips. She hated giving up the chance for a good argument, but her mom did have the right idea. It was time to have some fun!

"I've just got to run to my locker," Melanie said, remembering her backpack. As her parents headed for the car, she dashed up the school steps and bumped right into the mock-trial judge.

"Ms. Porter, well done," the judge said. "I'm truly impressed."

Melanie beamed. "Wow, thank you, Your Honor."

"Your teacher mentioned that you're interested in my alma mater."

"Georgetown. Yes, sir, they're so strong in international relations. I speak some Japanese and—" Melanie stopped abruptly and shook her head. "Actually, it doesn't matter. I was wait-listed, which is the academic equivalent of a guy saying he just wants to be friends." She tried to laugh it off, but it was clear she was upset.

"I'm sorry to hear that," the judge said.

"Don't be." Melanie shrugged. "I'm going to Northwestern. Great school, and just forty minutes from home."

"Come on, Melanie bear," James shouted from the parking lot. "Daddy's waiting!"

Melanie cringed with embarrassment. "How lucky am I?" she muttered.

The judge laughed and put a reassuring hand on her shoulder. "I have an old classmate who works in admissions at Georgetown. No guarantees, but I could give him a call if you'd like."

If she'd like? Melanie's eyes bugged at the man. A second later, she was hugging the life out of him.

"I'll take that as a *yes*," the judge croaked. "You're obstructing my airway."

CHAPTER TWO

Later that afternoon, Melanie's family was getting ready for dinner. As her dad prepared pork chops for the outdoor grill, her ten-year-old brother, Trey, strolled into the kitchen.

"Hey, big man," James said to his son, "your sister knocked it out of the park at the mock trial."

Trey frowned. "I'm glad somebody had a victory today."

"Everything all right?" James asked.

"Albert just beat me at chess again." Trey glanced down at Albert—who happened to be a potbellied pig. Albert snorted with glee.

"Stop gloating," Trey told his pet. Then he turned to his mom and held up a beaker. "I need thirteen cubic centimeters of orange juice, please."

Michelle filled the beaker with juice and handed it back to her son.

"Thank you, Mother," Trey replied and headed out of the kitchen.

James exchanged a glance with his wife.

"He's just going through a phase," Michelle assured her husband.

James rolled his eyes. "A 'phase' is when he wants to be a cowboy. I'm telling you, Trey's got *issues*."

"Kids with high IQs have big imaginations," Michelle said. "We need to encourage him. Besides, you're the one who said a pet would teach him responsibility."

"Yeah. I *meant*, get a puppy, not turn our place into a pigsty." As James continued seasoning the pork chops, he noticed Albert glaring at him.

James frowned down at the little pig. "And he keeps eyeballing me like I'm cooking his cousin!"

Her back to him, Michelle laughed. "He's not eyeballing you, James."

"He's doing it right now. Look!" James pointed. But the second Michelle turned to look, Albert lowered his head.

"See? Nothing," Michelle said. "All in your head."

An hour or so later, the Porters greeted their dinner guests—Officer O'Malley and his wife, Emma. Mr. O'Malley was James's deputy officer and good friend.

"You look wonderful, Emma," Michelle told the very pregnant Mrs. O'Malley.

"Really?" Mrs. O'Malley replied, waddling into the living room, "'Cuz I feel like a house!"

In a corner of the room, Trey was busy conducting another one of his weird experiments. With thick rubber gloves on his hands, he poured a bright blue liquid onto a drooping potted plant. In seconds, the nearly dead plant began to perk up.

Nobody noticed. All eyes were focused on the young woman descending the stairs.

"Hey!" Mr. O'Malley waved to Melanie. "There's our superstar."

Melanie smiled politely at her parents' dinner guests. "Hey, Mr. and Mrs. O'Malley. Sorry I won't be joining you."

"Celebrating, I hope," Mr. O'Malley replied. "Wild party?"

Melanie tugged on her baggy clothes. "Yeah, I'm hanging out with a couple of mock-trial friends at the library. We're going to debate jury-selection strategies."

James nodded his approval. "That's my baby."

Honk! Honk! Honk!

"And that's my cue. Have a great night, guys!" Melanie called. Before she could get out the door, however, her dad stepped forward to block her way. "See you by curfew," Melanie assured him. "*Of course.*"

James grinned and stepped aside.

Shaking her head, Melanie jogged down the front-porch steps. She didn't have to turn around to know her father was still standing at the door, watching her. She ducked into the awaiting car and greeted her two best friends, Katie and Nancy.

The girls waved sweetly at Melanie's dad. But the second James closed the door, their plastic grins fell.

"All clear," Katie announced.

Melanie shook her head. "Nope . . . wait for the second wave."

Sure enough, James opened the front door again

11

and waved for a second time. He closed the door, and Katie was about to speak again, but Melanie held up her hand.

"Now here comes the curtain," she warned.

As if on cue, James peeked out from behind one side of the window curtains. A second later, the fabric stopped moving, and Melanie exhaled.

"*Now* we're good!"

She quickly stripped off her baggy clothes to reveal a low-necked, hip-hugging ensemble. Katie and Nancy whooped, and the girls drove off.

Hunter's mock-trial party was off the hook! Kids were hanging on the lawn and dancing in the living room. There were balloons and confetti and a great big cake. Everyone greeted Melanie with shouts and backslaps as she and her best friends made their way into the kitchen to get sodas.

The whole night was like a dream. Hunter even danced with her and gave her that totally overdue hug. But Melanie couldn't shake the feeling her father was watching. When Katie suggested she could have tried telling her dad the truth, Melanie laughed.

"Are you kidding?" she choked. "The man is completely rigid. He still treats me like I'm a little girl. He doesn't even want me to wear perfume because he thinks it sends out the wrong message!"

Katie put a hand on Melanie's shoulder. "You clearly need to take your mind off things and come on our college tour this weekend. Saturday, we're staying with my sister at her sorority at Pitt."

Nancy nodded with enthusiasm. "And we can even hit Georgetown one day—it's not that far."

"Thanks," Melanie said, "but my dad would never let me go with you guys. Besides, it'd be like having a taste of something you love, knowing you might never get it."

Nancy sighed and nodded. "Like when Katie tried on those limited-edition Manolo Blahniks."

Hours later, Melanie waltzed into her house, back undercover. "Well, hello," she called to her dad.

James nodded his approval at his daughter's oversize sweatshirt and baggy jeans. "How was the library, sweetie?"

"Out of control," Melanie said flatly.

Just then, James noticed something on Melanie's

head. "What's in your hair?"

Melanie put a hand to her head. Oops, she thought, feeling the confetti from the party. She gulped, talking fast as she edged toward the stairs. "We went a little crazy with the paper shredder at the library, but don't worry . . . we recycled it for the St. Patrick's Day parade. Good night!"

Before her dad could start grilling her, Melanie raced up the stairs and slammed her bedroom door. She hit the sack soon after, and so did the rest of her family.

The night passed peacefully. The sunrise brought a quiet chirping of birdsong. A slight breeze stirred the air, but the whole world still seemed completely serene until—

"Aaaaaaaaaaiiieeeeee!"

Melanie's father sat bolt upright. Flailing frantically, the police chief became tangled in his bedcovers and fell to the floor with a loud thud. He scrambled for his baseball bat and raced to the living room, where he found Melanie fully dressed, jumping up and down. She screamed again and pointed to the telephone answering machine.

14

Trey ran up behind his dad. Apparently worried that nuclear fallout might be in play, he held a Geiger counter up to the voice recorder.

"Melanie, what is it?" her mom cried, rushing up behind James and Trey.

Melanie sputtered and pointed at the answering machine again. Too excited to explain, she simply pressed the PLAY button.

"Ms. Porter," a deep voice began. "It's Judge Mehagian calling. As it happens, the Georgetown admissions committee is interviewing a select few wait-list candidates. No promises, but if you can find your way to D.C. by four p.m. this Monday, I have a feeling your commute will be a lot longer than forty minutes this fall. Congratulations and have a lovely trip."

Now Melanie's mom was screaming and jumping up and down. Trey shouted and pumped a fist into the air. Even little Albert began to run around in excited circles. Only Melanie's dad remained stock-still.

When everyone finally quieted down, Melanie turned to her little brother. "Why are *you* so happy?"

"I'm going to turn your room into a science lab!" Trey cried, pumping his fist again.

"It's all yours, baby brother!" Melanie laughed and turned to her mom. "We've got three days to get to Washington. We should totally drive there. Make a trip of it—"

"Trip?" James interrupted, finally snapping to life. "What trip?"

Nobody answered James. Instead, Michelle struck her forehead, suddenly remembering. "Oh, Melanie, I've got two big open houses this weekend."

Melanie frowned and studied the carpet a moment. Then her eyes brightened. "Wait, Katie and Nancy can take me! They're already headed out for a college tour tomorrow. They'll just be a few hours from D.C."

"Oh, that's perfect," her mom said with a grin. "Problem solved. I'm so proud of you, sweetie!"

Melanie and her mom hugged.

Honk! Honk Honk!

"That's Katie!" Melanie broke from her mom and headed for the door. "She's going to lose it when I tell her! I'm going to Georgetown!"

Melanie's mother waved good-bye and headed for the bedroom. James followed his wife with a scowl on his face.

16

"'Perfect?'" he snapped. "'Problem solved?' What happened to our big plan? We agreed on Northwestern. Did you even know she applied to Georgetown?"

Michelle nodded her head as she selected a suit from the closet. "I helped her fill out the application."

"What?" James threw up his hands. "Whose side are you on?"

"Both of yours," she said while changing.

James huffed. "That's impossible."

"Georgetown is a great school," Michelle insisted.

"We don't know anyone there," James said, still trying to wrap his head around this development. "How would she even begin to take care of herself?"

"Because you're an amazing father." Michelle smiled and patted her husband's shoulder. "You showed her right from wrong. You taught her how to think for herself and be strong. She's ready for this because of you."

James shook his head. "Nice try. But you and I both know there's nothing nice out there."

Michelle sighed. She finished getting ready, then grabbed her car keys and headed for the door. "I know this is hard for you, but she's not a little girl anymore. You've got to relax. . . ."

But James couldn't relax. All day at the police station, he continued to stew, until he finally thought of a solution—the perfect solution.

CHAPTER THREE

"Road trip! Road trip! Road trip!" Melanie chanted with Katie and Nancy as they drove down her street later that afternoon. With school out for the weekend, the girls were free and ready to roll to Georgetown.

"So let's hit the road really early tomorrow," Melanie told her best friends. Then she squealed. "I can't believe this is actually happening!"

Behind the wheel, Katie nodded. "I can't believe your dad's actually *allowing* it to happen."

Nancy shook her head. "It seems like just

yesterday he was driving you and Jack Cole to prom in the back of his squad car."

"Or planting that tracking device in your sneaker," Katie added.

Melanie shuddered at the memories. "Ladies, it took me seventeen years, but I think I finally got through to the man: you can be 'chief' at the station, but you've got to be 'dad' at home."

As Katie pulled her car into the Porters' driveway, the girls laughed. But their laughter instantly died when they saw what was waiting for Melanie. James stood next to his Fox Springs police vehicle. A handwritten sign on the back of the big, white SUV read: GEORGETOWN EXPRESS.

"Oh, no," Melanie said. She had a bad feeling about this.

A second later, James waved at Melanie and erased all doubt. "Road trip! Road trip! Road trip!" he chanted.

"This is crazy!" Melanie complained to her mother. "Have you seen what we're driving? It'll be like a thousand mile ride-along! Why is Dad doing this?"

Michelle glanced out the window at her husband

and sighed. "Because he loves you and wants to spend time with you."

"That is so cruel!" Melanie wailed.

Melanie's mom seemed genuinely sorry. She paced back and forth and finally faced her daughter. "Tell me . . . *what* would make it less painful?"

Melanie's eyes widened. She knew just the thing.

"You said she could stay at a sorority house?" James howled to his wife later that evening. "What next? Are you going to tie raw meat to her back and send her out in the woods!"

Michelle rolled her eyes as she turned down the bedcovers. "Her friends are going to be with Katie's sister at Pitt. It's right near your mom's, where you're already planning to stay."

"This is daddy-daughter time, Michelle," James insisted, throwing up his hands. "I've got a lot planned for us. I shouldn't have to share."

Hands on hips, Michelle glared at her husband. "Why are you taking this trip, James?"

James folded his arms and glared right back. "I told you. To support Melanie."

"Good," Michelle replied, "because if you were

doing it out of some misguided notion that in *three* days you and your daughter will do so much bonding that she won't want to go away to school—that would be a bad reason."

James's frown deepened. He turned to leave the bedroom and noticed Trey at the door. The boy entered and held out a piece of paper.

"Dad, since you're going to Washington, I need you to take a message to the secretary of defense."

James took the note and read it aloud. "'I have devised a means to create a subspecies of superpigs who, in the future, will defend the country from our enemies.'" James sighed. Then he handed the note back to his son. "You should get it to him yourself. And you may want to housebreak your pig first."

Trey shrugged. "Done."

Since when? James was about to ask when he heard the sound of a toilet flushing. A moment later, Trey's little potbellied pig trotted out of the bathroom. Trey tossed his dad a proud smile. Then he and Albert strolled away.

The next morning, Melanie dragged herself out of bed, washed up, and dressed for the big trip. She couldn't believe her girlfriends wouldn't be picking her up. Glancing out the window, she shuddered at the alternative—her dad's totally embarrassing police SUV. She noticed her mom and dad in the driveway talking.

"Where's Trey?" her dad was asking as he finished packing the vehicle.

"He left an hour ago for science club," her mom replied. "It's an all-day field trip. So I'm picking him up after work."

Melanie went downstairs and out the front door. She lingered on the porch as her mom and dad said their good-byes. Then she approached the driveway, and her mom gave her a hug.

"Let's go, Melanie Bear!" her dad shouted, already behind the wheel.

James started the car, and Melanie climbed into the passenger side. Her mom waved, and Melanie pressed her face against the window to mouth a single final word: *Help!*

It didn't work.

Her dad rolled out of their neighborhood and headed for the highway. Stopping at a traffic light, he turned to Melanie.

"Isn't this exciting?!" he asked with a big grin.

Melanie didn't answer.

"I made us a little road kit." Her dad grabbed a bag from the backseat. "Take a look. . . ."

Melanie poked through the bag and frowned. "Beef jerky?"

"Only the finest," James winked. "I've got some Hubba Bubba, Chips Ahoy, and Doritos family-size."

Melanie rolled her eyes. "What if I don't want to *be* family size?"

"Come on," James said. "This is classic road trip food. You've been to a truck stop?"

"Yeah." Melanie smirked. "But *you* never let me out of the car."

"Let's see what else we've got. . . ." James pawed through the bag himself. He held up a CD.

Melanie read the home-mixed label: "Daddy/ Daughter Groove Machine?"

James nodded. "'Double Dutch Bus.' We used to sing it in the car all the time." Outside, the traffic light turned green. James put the CD in the player and started driving again.

"Double Dutch Bus" began to play. James drove along, bopping his head to the happy beat. He glanced at Melanie and grinned.

"Remember?" he asked.

Melanie folded her arms and scowled. "Nope. Doesn't ring a bell."

"Come on," James coaxed. "This was our song."

Melanie looked away. "Sorry."

James sighed. "It's okay. We can just talk."

"Talk?" Melanie glanced back at her dad. "About what?"

"You know—father-daughter talks," James said with great seriousness. "We're gonna get deep. I just hope seven hundred miles gives us enough time. . . ."

Six minutes later, Melanie and her dad were sitting in total silence. They'd run out of conversation.

Melanie searched her brain for a topic that she and her dad might be able to discuss. But she came up with *nada*. Zippo. Nothing. Melanie exhaled.

"What?" James asked.

"What?" Melanie replied.

"Oh," James said, "I thought you said something."

"No."

"Oh?" James said. "I just heard a noise."

Melanie rolled her eyes. "I was exhaling."

"Oh, right." James began tapping his fingers on the

steering wheel. After another ten minutes of silence, James glanced at his daughter. "I spy a mailbox."

"Huh?" Melanie said.

James grinned and tipped his head toward the window. "I spy a green Volkswagen."

Melanie sighed.

Ten minutes later, her dad was belting out: "B-I-N-G-O! B-I-N-G-O! And Bingo was his name-O!"

This was going to be a *very* long trip.

"Okay, guess how far we've gone now?" James asked after another ten minutes.

"One million miles," Melanie said flatly.

"Wrong!" Her dad pointed to the odometer. "We've gone forty-three miles!" He grinned. "Okay, guess how long we've been driving?"

"Forever."

"Wrong! Forty minutes." He laughed. "Is this fun or what?"

Melanie forced a smile, until she saw the sign ahead: *Northwestern*. Her dad turned off the highway.

"Oh, my goodness, look where we are," James said in a totally fake tone of surprise.

"What are you doing?" Melanie cried.

"Nothing." James gave an innocent shrug. "What's the problem?

"I thought this was the *Georgetown Express*!"

"You have to see more than one college on a college road trip," James said. "What's the harm, right?"

"The harm is that we've got a lot of ground to cover today," Melanie snapped, "and I've already seen Northwestern!"

"Not as a potential student," her father said. "Come on . . . flow with me, flow with me."

CHAPTER FOUR

"Look at this place!" James exclaimed. "The trees, the fields. It's like a four-star resort with some books and learning."

Melanie glanced around the sunny campus. She instantly recognized visiting high school students and their parents by the dazed and confused looks on their faces—that and the HELLO MY NAME IS tags on their jackets and shirts.

"Just please don't embarrass me," she told her father.

"How could I embarrass you?" James asked.

Melanie quickly found out.

At the campus bookstore, James bought a Northwestern sweatshirt, a *Go Cats* ball cap, and a bright purple scarf that matched the team colors. When he stepped out of the store clad in his new gear, Melanie rolled her eyes

James waved a giant foam finger at some passing students and shouted, "Whooee! Go Cats! Number one, baby! Purple passion, you know what I'm sayin'!"

Melanie hid her face, pretending she didn't know the man.

Fifteen minutes later, they were back on the quad green. A student guide was holding a question-and-answer session, and James insisted they join the group—as part of the "experience."

Grinning excitedly, one parent raised his hand.

"Hi! Doug Greenhut," he said brightly, pointing to his tag. "I'm a BPT—'booster parent in training' up here from Orlando on our big college road trip. This is my daughter, Wendy."

"Wendy Greenhut: CST. That's 'college student in training,'" she chirped.

The student guide tried not to cringe. "Did you have a question?"

Still grinning, Doug spoke. "I was wondering when parents' weekend is?"

"Early November," the guide replied.

"What?" Doug looked stricken. "That's *three* months after school starts!"

Wendy's smile turned upside down. "I don't want to go that long without seeing you, Dad."

"We'll talk every day. I promise," her father cooed.

Wendy whooped and the two shared a father-daughter high five.

The student guide rolled his eyes. "Okay, if there are any other questions we may have to wave the 'no tipping' rule."

James tried to raise his hand, but Melanie grabbed it. Before she could stop him, her father raised his other hand—the one wearing the foam finger.

Melanie groaned and covered her eyes.

"Yes, Mr. School Spirit, with the foam finger. What's your question?" the student guide asked.

"How does Northwestern compare to other universities like *Georgetown*, for example?" James asked.

"I'd say we're as good as Georgetown, if not better," the guide replied.

James nodded. "So hypothetically, if your

daughter got into Northwestern and could go there for less money, given the savings on plane fare, you'd send her to Northwestern, right?"

The guide nodded. "Absolutely."

James faced his daughter. "See? He's smart. They've got smart kids here. You'll fit right in."

Melanie narrowed her eyes. "Excuse me," she spoke up, "but what if, *hypothetically*, your dad was an overprotective control freak who lived forty minutes from Northwestern? *Then* would you go to Georgetown?"

The whole group had an answer: "Yes! Without question!"

James pointed an accusing foam finger at the crowd. "Who said that? Who? Who?"

"I knew this was a bad idea," Melanie mumbled. She turned to walk away and tripped right over a guy who'd stopped to tie his shoe. "Yikes!" Melanie yelped.

"I'm so sorry about that," the guy said sweetly. "Are you okay?"

"I'm fine . . ." Melanie began. But her voice trailed off when she actually got a look at the guy she'd tripped over. He was tall and muscular with a dreamy smile—a total hottie.

"Th-thanks," she stammered.

"I'm Nick," said the boy, holding her gaze. "I don't think I've seen you around before."

"Actually, I'm just checking out the campus. I'm Melanie." She offered her hand and he shook it. She was about to pull it back again, but he held on.

"So, what's the verdict?" Nick said with a teasing smile. "Do you like what you see?"

Ohmigosh, she thought, her knees turning to jelly. "Uh-huh," she whispered, then caught herself. "I mean, the *campus* is very nice."

"Hey, listen," Nick said, checking his watch. "I've got a free hour before my next class. How about a personal tour?"

Suddenly a wall of purple appeared between them, breaking their hands apart. "Personal tour of *what*?" James demanded.

Here we go again, Melanie thought. Party over by order of the chief of police.

"Dad, this is Nick," she said in a resigned tone of disappointment. "Nick, my dad."

Nick smiled and pumped James's hand. "Pleasure to meet you, sir. I was about to show Melanie around campus . . . that is, with your permission, sir."

Go ahead and be polite, Melanie thought with a sigh. It won't do any good.

"I don't have a problem with that," James replied.

Melanie blinked. "Did you hit your head?" she asked her father.

"I trust you," her dad replied. "Besides, there's just something about this school that feels safe. Meet me at the student union when you're done. You kids have fun."

James reached into his pocket and offered them a fistful of dollar bills. "Ice-cream cones on me!" he declared.

My dad has been replaced by a pod person, Melanie thought, scratching her head.

James waved good-bye with his big foam finger.

"Wow," Nick gushed. "I wish my dad was that cool. Shall we go?"

Melanie shrugged and took his arm. "I'm all yours! I mean, lead the way."

Nick took her all around the campus. Finally, he showed her a building that was larger than her high school and about as crowded.

"I can't believe that's just a law library," Melanie said.

Nick nodded proudly. "I'm telling you . . . this campus is fantastic."

Melanie sighed. "I know it's a great school, but I sort of wanted to get farther away from the nest." *And by nest I mean my father,* she wanted to add.

Nick nodded. "I hear you, but the way I look at it, you have your whole life to do that. My parents live less than an hour away and it's awesome. I have a place to cram for exams when I need privacy, free laundry, home-cooked meals whenever I want. I've got the best of both worlds."

"Now you're starting to sound like my dad," Melanie said.

"Well," Nick said with a shrug. "The chief's a pretty smart guy."

Melanie froze. *Chief?* She narrowed her eyes suspiciously at Nick. "You know, I'd sure love an iced tea."

Nick winked. "Be right back."

As soon as Nick was gone, Melanie's smile vanished. "Chief?" she repeated. *Now how would Nick know that her dad was a police chief?*

"Arrrrrgh!" she cried as it hit her. "No wonder he had no problem sending me off with a strange

34

boy," she muttered. Nick wasn't a stranger at all!

Furious, Melanie scanned the campus. She spied her father across the lawn, talking to a pair of campus security officers.

Okay, chief, she thought. Two can play your lame little game!

James was feeling good. He knew his rookie would convince Melanie to go to Northwestern. And since he was sure his daughter would be attending school here in the fall, it made sense to grill a couple of guards about campus security.

"What do you do if you encounter an individual resisting arrest?" he asked.

One guard tapped an electronic device strapped to his belt. "We have Tasers," he said.

Amateurs, James thought, rolling his eyes. "Forget about a Taser! That's not going to hurt a *real* criminal."

Before he could launch into a lecture on crime fighting, James felt his daughter's hand on his arm. He turned to find Melanie grinning up at him.

"Well," he said with raised eyebrows, "looks like somebody's having a good time."

Melanie's head bobbed excitedly. "Not a good time. The best time *ever*! This place is *awesome*!"

James nodded, feeling very pleased with himself for selecting Nick out of all the rookies under his command. Good job, son, he thought. I can't wait to thank you for making sure my little baby chick nests close to home.

"See?" James told his daughter. "What have I been trying to tell you?"

"Yeah." Melanie nodded. "First Nick took me to see the library, and then he took me to a frat party!"

James's smile disappeared. "Frat party?"

"Yeah!" Melanie nodded, eyes wide. "Everyone was in bikinis dancing in a kiddie pool. It was *cray-zee*! No one goes to class. A party in the middle of the day. Really easy to make curfew that way. Northwestern is what's up!"

James felt his blood pressure rising. He looked around. "Where is Nick?"

"I'm not sure," Melanie said. "He hurt himself doing the *wuuuuuurm*."

Imitating a dance move, Melanie bumped her dad with her swaying hip.

Suddenly, Nick appeared, clutching a tall glass of

iced tea. "Hey, Melanie, I've got a drink here with your name on it!"

The chief's eyes bugged. In a near-crazed state, James snatched the Taser from the security guard's belt and zapped his rookie.

"Aaaahhh!" Nick howled, dropping to the grass.

CHAPTER FIVE

After the paramedics treated Nick, James and Melanie returned to the SUV and took to the road again. But when James tried to start a conversation, Melanie ignored him. She was still stewing about the way her father had tried to trick her into giving up on Georgetown.

After several more miles of angry silence, Melanie noticed her father opening his cell phone to make a call.

The phone rang back in their hometown, where Michelle was busy with her real-estate clients. She excused herself when she heard her cell phone.

"I just called to check in," James told his wife when she picked up.

"So we're good?" Michelle asked.

"All good," James replied. "Melanie's having a great time."

In the passenger seat, Melanie harrumphed and whipped out her own cell phone.

"We met a lot of interesting people at Northwestern," James continued.

"That's great," Michelle replied, smiling. Then her call-waiting beep sounded. "Just a second. I have another call."

She put her husband on hold and answered. "Hello?"

"Mom, you're never going to believe what Dad did!" Melanie cried.

Still on hold, James glanced across the car seat to find Melanie on the phone, too!

"I'm innocent of everything," James yelled into his cell. Then he turned to his daughter. "Hang up!"

"I object!" Melanie cried.

"And I overrule!" James shot back.

"Stop arguing!" Michelle cried from the other end of the line. By now, she had connected the two calls. "Both of you listen to me—"

"But Mom, Dad's bugging me more than anyone in the history of people!"

"Wow, that much?" Melanie's mom said. Then she glanced at her real-estate clients. The couple appeared to be getting impatient. "Look, you two," she told her daughter and husband. "I'll call you back later."

After Michelle hung up, James turned and glared at his daughter. "No one likes a snitch," he snapped.

Melanie squinted. "What happened to 'always tell the truth even if people don't like you for it'?"

James frowned. "That was a different lesson."

"Why do I need so many lessons?" Melanie wailed. "I've been a good kid. I listen to you and Mom. I do well in school. The worst thing I've ever done is go dance with my friends at a party!"

"Party?" James's eyes widened. "When did you go to a party?"

Luckily, just then, Melanie's cell phone went off.

James tensed. "If that's Mom again, tell her we're having a good time."

"Hello?" Melanie said, shooting her father a look as she answered. She was greeted by blaring music and the telltale crunch of junk food.

"Oh. My. Gosh." Nancy gushed between bites. "The cutest guy just drove by! And Katie was like 'oooh,' and he was like 'ahhhh,' and I was like 'whatever'! So how's family bonding?"

Melanie snorted. "It's great. We just paid a visit to Northwestern and my dad Tasered one of his own deputies. He's really kicking it up a notch, right?" Melanie covered the phone and turned to her father. "Nancy says 'congratulations.'"

James rolled his eyes.

"No, he can't hear you," Melanie assured Nancy. She listened for a moment. Then she began to laugh. "I know, I know," Melanie cried, glancing sideways at her father.

The conversation continued like that for the next hour. All through it, James seemed to shrink behind the steering wheel.

Finally, Melanie's conversation was interrupted by a loud beep. On her cell phone, the low-battery indicator flashed red.

"Oh, shoot, my battery's almost out," she muttered.

Her dad hid a relieved smile. But it vanished

when Melanie yanked a power adapter out of her purse and plugged it into the dashboard.

"Okay, I'm good," she said to Nancy. "So, where were we?"

"I know!" Melanie cried into her cell an hour later.

James checked his watch. Two hours of giggles, gossip, and fashion tips, courtesy of Melanie and her friends.

Just when he thought it couldn't get worse, James had to put on the brakes as traffic on the interstate slowed to a crawl. Melanie finally ended her call and gazed apprehensively through the windshield. They crept along for a moment, until they both spotted the warning sign: ROAD CONSTRUCTION NEXT 20 MILES.

"Twenty miles?" Melanie cried. She was supposed to meet the girls at Pitt! "No way I'm going to make it at this rate. We're just going to have to use the siren."

"What? Absolutely not," James said. "Nobody touches my siren."

"Desperate times call for desperate measures, Dad."

"Melanie, getting to a slumber party is not an

emergency," James replied seriously. "Now reach in my bag and get me P-GIPS."

Melanie blinked. "What's 'peejips'?"

"Police Global Positioning System," James proudly announced.

"Why don't you just say, Police GPS?" Melanie asked as she fished out the device.

Ignoring his daughter's question, James grabbed the GPS unit. He quickly activated the system. "P-GIPS, route fastest time to I-23," he asked the device.

"Calculating distance to I-23," a robotic voice replied. "For fastest route to I-23, exit highway in one mile."

"Thank you, P-GIPS," James said with a glance at his daughter that said, *Aren't-you-impressed?*

Melanie rolled her eyes.

Fifteen minutes later, the SUV turned onto a dirt road.

"At the next intersection, turn right," the P-GIPS system said.

James drove forward, searching desperately for an intersection—or even a paved road!

"At the next intersection, turn right. At the next intersection turn right," the P-GIPS system repeated.

Melanie looked up from the map she had optimistically opened. "Dad, I think P-GIPS is broken. The map says we need to turn back."

James frowned. "Are you going to believe a piece of paper or a forty million dollar satellite? I bet Grandma's house is right around the corner."

Suddenly, the P-GIPS went crazy. "*Achtung! Achtung!*" it cried. Then the device suddenly switched tones. "You have selected three tickets to *Lost in America*. To find the theater nearest you, press one."

Taking his eyes off the road for a split second, James shook the P-GIPS device.

Ker-plump!

The front tire plowed into a deep pit in the road. The SUV bounced once. Then Melanie and James heard a loud *pop* as the tire exploded and the SUV came to a stop.

Melanie glanced around at the dense forest that surrounded them. From somewhere not too far away, a coyote howled. "I like what Grandma's done with the place."

With a groan of frustration, James climbed out of the SUV. He examined the tire. "Don't worry," he called, "I'll have this fixed and we'll be back on the . . ." He paused to look around. ". . . tiny dirt path in no time."

James walked to the back of the SUV and opened the hatchback. Then he turned the knob that unlocked the storage compartment.

The squeal of a pig greeted him.

"What the . . ." James frowned into the cramped space. The SUV's storage compartment had been transformed into a mini biodome stocked with packets of astronaut food, books, a laptop, a water dispenser, and an air-circulation system.

"Trey!" James cried when he saw his son. "What are you doing?"

"Going to D.C.," Trey replied. "You told me to take my note to the secretary of defense myself!"

James slapped his own forehead. "Have you been hiding in here the whole time? You could have suffocated!"

Trey grinned and shook his head. "No way. I built an air-ventilation system. I could've survived for weeks."

45

Albert gave a little pig grunt.

"Sorry, Albert," Trey said. "I mean *we* could've survived."

James shook his finger. "You'll be lucky to survive into next week when your mother and I get through with you. . . ." He pulled out his cell phone to call Michelle. "No service," he muttered, then fixed his son with a glare. "You just bought yourself a stay of execution."

With a sigh, James went about setting up the automatic jack. He turned it on, and the front of the SUV began to rise. Melanie touched her father's shoulder and gestured to her brother. Trey was crawling around on the ground, studying plant life with a magnifying glass.

"What are we going to do with him, Dad?" she whispered. "I have the biggest interview of my life, and I'd prefer to do it without Doctor Evil and Franken-pig along for the ride."

The automatic jack was still humming away. It continued to lift the shattered tire out of the pothole.

James faced his daughter. "What choice do we have, Melanie? We're in the middle of nowhere."

"Can't we leave him here?" she pleaded. "Maybe

46

a nice family of wolves will adopt him."

James shook his head, and Melanie peered over her dad's shoulder.

"Dad, the car!" Melanie shouted. The jack was still lifting the SUV—and the vehicle was about to tip over!

James turned and lunged for the automatic jack. He flipped the power off, and the SUV teetered on the edge of the road. Then James turned another switch and the jack began to lower the car.

"Wow," Melanie said. "That could've been bad."

Her father shook his head. "Not on my watch. James Porter puts the *S* in safety!"

Just then, the loose dirt on the side of the road gave way. The SUV lurched to the side, flipped over, and rolled down the deep ravine beside the road. It finally came to a stop on its side.

James, Melanie, and Trey raced to the edge of the road and stared down at their upended vehicle.

"You don't see that every day," Melanie murmured.

Just then, they heard a familiar sound. It was the robotic voice of the P-GIPS. "At the next inter-section, turn right. . . ."

CHAPTER SIX

Down in the ravine, James tried desperately to rock the SUV back onto its wheels.

"Dad, what are you doing?" Melanie called.

Huffing and puffing, James paused. "I'm going to rock this thing over and we'll be on our way. I just need a little momentum. One, two, three!"

James pushed with all his might. Melanie and Trey watched him in disbelief. A loud crack echoed through the ravine, and their dad clutched his back.

"Something popped! Something popped," he cried.

"Do you need that man girdle thingy you wear?" Melanie asked.

Trey scratched his head. "I thought that was Mom's."

James rose to his full height and his back snapped back to normal. He shot his kids an angry look. Suddenly, Albert began to squeal, loud enough to shake the birds out of the trees.

Still clutching his back, James frowned: "Now what's *his* problem?"

"I think he hears something," Trey said, bending low. "What is it, Albert?" he whispered to the pig. "Do you hear something? Is it trouble?"

Albert squealed again.

"Is it fire?" Trey asked. "Is Jimmy stuck in the well?"

James scratched his head. "Is Jimmy stuck in the *what*?"

Melanie rolled her eyes. "Trey's been watching a lot of *Lassie* reruns."

"It's research!" Trey said.

James shook his head and climbed to the top of a high boulder. Shielding his eyes from the setting sun, he scanned the forest around them.

"I think I see a road over there," James called to his kids. He tapped his head. "See, natural sense of direction!"

"Albert was right!" Trey cried.

49

"Whatever," James said, his eyes on the distant road. "I'm going out there. No matter what happens, you do not move from the spot, you got it? There is nothing nice out here."

Melanie sat down on a rock. "Message taken, Dad. We're not going anywhere."

James took off through the woods and quickly became lost. As he struggled through some brush, he began muttering to himself. "'Is Jimmy stuck in the well?'" He shook his head. "That boy needs to make some friends. Friends that aren't pigs!"

Finally, James found a cleared path, which led to a paved road. Even better, he spotted a battered pick-up truck parked on the shoulder.

Excited, James ran to the truck, looking around for its owner.

"Hello? Anybody home?" he yelled.

He noticed a GONE FISHIN' sticker attached to the battered bumper. After yelling a few more times, James looked inside the truck and spied a CB radio.

I can call for help, he realized. James tried the door. It was unlocked! Climbing into the driver's seat, he reached for the CB's receiver. But before he could turn the unit on, a strong hand took hold of him and yanked hard.

"Whoa!" James felt himself being dragged out of the vehicle.

Thud! Landing flat on his back, he looked up to find two men standing over him. One man was short, with a funny face, a straw hat, and a fisherman's vest. The other one was huge, practically a giant.

The giant glared down at James and scratched his unshaven chin with a metal hook that took the place of his right hand.

Uh-oh. James gulped, then grinned like an idiot. "I bet you're wondering what I was doing in your truck."

The little man, whose name was Dave, scowled. "Saw you reaching under the dash. We have a pretty good idea."

The giant, Nud, nodded in agreement.

"I was just trying to borrow your CB," James explained.

"Along with my wallet?" Dave snapped.

"Wallet?" James sat up and glanced back inside the truck. For the first time, he noticed the wallet sitting on the front seat. *Dang.* "Look," James said quickly, "this is all just one big misunderstanding. I'm a police officer."

"Where's your badge?" Dave demanded.

James patted his pants pockets. "It's right . . ." Suddenly, he remembered he'd left his wallet and badge in his jacket—and his jacket was inside the SUV!

"Actually, I left it in the car," James said, carefully rising to his feet. "I'll go get it . . ."

Dave shook his head. "I don't think so."

Nud grunted in agreement and began to move closer to James. James acted fast. He snatched a log off the ground and waved it in front of him.

"This is your last warning," James threatened the giant. "That looks like an expensive hook. You don't want to bend it."

Nud charged. James swung the log. The giant caught it, yanked it out of his hand, and cracked the thick wood in two.

James was in serious trouble.

The big man's hook came at him. James braced himself, certain he was done for. And then—

"Stop!" a loud voice shouted. "Stop in the name of the law!"

The big man froze, hook in the air, and everyone turned to see Melanie Porter standing there, legs braced. She was wearing her father's police jacket and holding his badge high.

"Step away from the prisoner!" Melanie commanded.

"Prisoner?" Dave asked.

Melanie nodded and strode up to the two men. "Are you all right?" she asked them.

"Are *they* all right?" James cried.

"Silence," Melanie ordered. Then she whispered, "Just flow with me, Dad."

Taking out her father's handcuffs, she raised her voice again. "You are in the presence of one of the most malicious, malevolent criminals you'll ever see!"

With gaping mouths, the two fishermen watched Melanie cuff James.

"You mean this guy?" Dave asked doubtfully.

Melanie nodded. "*This guy* has a list of priors a mile long! Robbery, forgery, and . . . hiring an impostor to pose as a college tour guide." She paused on that last charge to smirk at her father. "Goes by the name of James Porter, but most people call him Big Daddy."

"Yeah . . ." The little man bobbed his head. "I think I've heard of him!"

"That's right. She just saved your life," James roared, making his eye bug out. "I'm crazy! Real crazy!"

"I was escorting him to jail when my cruiser broke down," Melanie explained. "I'm going to need you to take us to town so I can call for backup."

"Happy to oblige, officer," Dave replied.

Just then, Trey and his pet pig arrived on the scene.

"We've got company," Dave said, pointing to the pair.

"Oh, yeah . . . um, they're with me," Melanie quickly explained. "Officer Albert, Pork Division—"

Albert squealed.

"And the boy is, uh . . . Jimmy," Melanie added. "The pig just saved him from a well."

The two fishermen glanced at each other and nodded. They were obviously very impressed.

Twenty minutes later, the fishermen's truck pulled up in front of a beautiful, rustic hotel in the middle of the forest. James and Melanie jumped out of the truck's cargo bay, followed by Trey with little Albert in his arms. James was still in handcuffs.

"Thanks for the lift," Melanie said, smiling at the two fishermen.

"No problem," said Nud.

By now, the two men had become pretty chummy with Melanie. They were even a little sweet on her. Big Nud grinned and saluted her, accidentally poking his forehead with his own hook. Wincing, he followed his little fishing buddy back to the truck.

After they drove off, Melanie took the cuffs off her dad. Then they headed toward the hotel, hauling their luggage with them.

"Nice work, baby girl," James said.

Melanie exhaled in relief. "You too, Dad."

James dropped his suitcase and gazed at the fancy hotel. "See? I told you everything was going to work out. This place looks nice."

But Albert snorted loudly and leaped out of Trey's arms. The little pig pressed his snout against a sign near the front door: NO PETS ALLOWED.

Melanie scratched her head. "Well, Trey, it looks like your little pig has to sleep outside."

"But Dad! Albert is a member of this family!" Trey protested.

"Not by blood," James said. "And this is the only hotel for thirty miles, we don't have a car, and I'm tired."

Albert squealed pathetically. He rolled over on the cold ground and pretended to shiver. Trey started to tear up.

James groaned. "Great. Got any ideas?"

Melanie tapped her chin. "I have a thought."

Five minutes later, Melanie, Trey, and their dad pushed through the glass doors of the hotel. Albert was now wrapped in a blanket and cradled in James's arms.

The Porters crossed the lobby and approached the front desk. But before they could address the manager, a man in a tuxedo cut them off. He strode right up to the woman behind the counter. At his side was a young woman in an over-the-top, way-too-frilly, wedding gown.

"Ms. Prince, I'm dumping a lot of coin on this wedding," the man said in an angry voice, "and I was told they'd be throwing rice at my little angel." He pointed to the young woman in the gown.

Behind the front desk, Ms. Prince frowned. "I'm sorry, Mr. Arcara," she said, "but it's against the law to throw rice. The birds might choke on it."

"Well, my daughter Lily might choke on her tears!" Mr. Arcara gestured to his daughter again.

"Princess Di had rice!" Lily wailed. "*I want my rice!*"

The hotel manager cleared her throat. "I'll see what I can do."

"Brown rice!" Lily noted. "I'm on a diet."

Ms. Prince nodded. "But of course you are."

When the pair finally marched away, James stepped up to the counter. "Hi, I'd like a couple rooms for the night."

Ms. Prince smiled. "How many are in your party?"

"Just me, the two kids, and the baby," James replied, gesturing to the blankets that swaddled Albert.

"Baby? Oh, I just love babies," Ms. Prince leaned over the counter and reached toward James. "Let me see the little angel!"

James leaped backward. "No, um . . . he has stranger anxiety. Been crying for hours. Don't want to disturb the other guests."

Albert snorted under the blanket.

Ms. Prince smiled. "Baby's getting hungry."

"I just gave you a bottle," James said to Albert.

The pig snorted again.

Ms. Prince looked at them curiously.

Melanie stepped up. "He's a real big eater!"

"Oh, *yeah*," James agreed, exchanging a glance with his kids. "He's kind of a *pig*."

"Okay, then," Ms. Prince said, turning her attention to a computer screen. "Let's see what rooms are available."

Score! Melanie thought. They were in!

CHAPTER SEVEN

There was only one vacancy at the hotel. The room was tiny, and it had an unimpressive view of the parking lot. Most of the space was taken up by two queen-sized beds, a dresser, and a television.

"Three hundred and fifty dollars for this!" James cried.

Melanie dropped her luggage. "If you need me, I'll be in the shower trying to wash this day off of me."

After Melanie disappeared into the bathroom, James's cell phone rang.

"It's Mom," James said, holding the phone out to

Trey. "She wants to talk to you."

Trey gulped. "Could you take a message?"

James shoved the phone into his son's hand.

"Hello," Trey squeaked.

"You are in big trouble!" Michelle cried, loud enough for James to hear. "I hope you know how to build a time machine, because you're not leaving the house again until the year 3000!"

"I'll draw up some plans with Albert," Trey said, "but I can't promise anything."

"This is the most dangerous thing you've ever done," Michelle went on. "I don't know what we're going to do with you, but we'll figure out something. You can believe that."

"Sorry, Mommy," Trey replied.

"I'll *think* about your apology," Michelle told her son. "Meanwhile, put me back on the phone with your dad."

Trey handed the phone back to James.

"So, you're all okay?" Michelle asked.

"I've got everything under control," he assured her.

"Really?" Michelle said. "Is that why when I called your mother she said you're not going to make it to her house tonight?"

James rolled his eyes. "We just had a little trouble with the car. We're at a nice hotel. We're going to get a good night's rest. Then we'll be right back on schedule."

Michelle let out a sigh. "How's daddy-daughter bonding?"

"Good," James said. "Trust me. Everything's going to be fine. I'll call you again."

A few minutes later, Melanie exited the bathroom, wearing a robe. A hotel towel was wrapped around her head.

"Albert, go start the bath," Trey commanded. The pig scurried off. A moment later, they heard the sound of running water. Trey rose and sauntered to the bathroom. "If you need us, we'll be in there playing chess," he announced.

Melanie sat on the bed and started brushing out her hair.

"How's it going?" James asked.

"I'm fine," Melanie said.

"I know you must be upset about missing the sleepover," James said. "For whatever it's worth, I was totally cool with it."

"Thanks, Dad," Melanie said, but she couldn't

hide her disappointment. "I should really start preparing for my interview now." She moved to the coffeemaker on the dresser. She tore open the package of preground coffee sitting beside it.

"What are you doing?" her father demanded.

Melanie shrugged. "Making coffee."

James snatched the bag from her hand. "You're not old enough to drink coffee. It'll stunt your growth."

"Dad, I'm seventeen. How tall do you want me to get?"

"Caffeine is a drug," James declared. "You do not take drugs. End of story. I'm going to dump it right now so you don't double back on me."

While Melanie watched in stunned silence, James poured the grounds into the trash can. "Why do you insist on treating me like a child?" she asked when he was done.

"Because, according to the law, you *are* one," her father replied.

With a frustrated groan, Melanie plopped onto one of the beds and opened her notebook. Trey and Albert emerged from the bathroom squeaky clean.

"I hope you left a towel for me," James said as he headed for the shower.

Melanie Porter is ready to leave home and head to college.

Melanie gets an interview at her number one college choice! And that means—road trip!

Melanie and her best friends can't wait to hit the road.

There is no way James Porter is going to let his
daughter out on the road unsupervised.

The road trip is on! But there is a catch. James
is driving!

Melanie could do without her father's support.

Along the road, James and Melanie make an
unplanned stop.

Melanie's younger brother, Trey, takes his pet pig for
a walk on the wild side.

Melanie, James, and Trey make it out of the woods.
But their troubles aren't over yet.

James and the family make a stop at Grandma
Porter's house.

Melanie arrives at her dream school. The only
problem? She is definitely not in her dream outfit!

James is determined to help his daughter make her interview.

Melanie got in! On the first day, the whole family comes to see her off.

He soon discovered all the towels had been used. Not only that, every inch of the counter was taken up with Melanie's girly stuff—brushes, skin creams, blow-dryer, eyeliner, lip gloss, hand cream.

James tucked his shaving kit on the only empty spot, the corner edge of the counter. Then he saw a bottle of perfume. He picked it up.

"Not my baby girl!" He set the perfume down and bumped into his shaving kit. *Plop!* It landed right in the toilet. "Noooo!" James cried.

Meanwhile, in the other room, Melanie heard her father's cry and looked up from her notes. Trey was sprawled out on the other bed watching *Lassie*, with Albert by his side. Soon, Trey dozed off, and Albert hopped off the bed and waddled over to the wastebasket. Snorting curiously, the pig stuck his wet snout into the can and started gobbling up the trashed coffee.

In the bathroom, James stepped out of the shower and wrapped a towel around his waist. He brushed his teeth and gargled with mouthwash. He spit—and heard someone pounding on the door.

"Just a minute," James yelled.

"Dad!" Trey cried frantically. "It's an emergency!"

63

The bathroom door opened and James stepped out, still wearing the towel. "Where's the fire?"

Trey looked up at his father with wide eyes. "There's something wrong with Albert."

James glanced at the pig and rubbed his eyes in disbelief. Albert was bouncing on the bed as if it were a trampoline. With each hop the little pig flew higher. Soon he was doing backflips and squealing with delight.

"What's up with him?" James asked.

Melanie pointed to the empty wastebasket. "He ate the coffee you threw out! All of it!"

"Squeeeeee!" squealed the supercaffeinated pig.

Just then, there was a knock at the door. "Yes?" James called.

A waiter barged into the room, a tray balanced on his shoulder. "Room service!" he declared.

"Squeeeeee!" Albert howled.

"Ahhhh!" screamed the surprised waiter.

Albert leaped through the open door and ran down the hall.

"Albert, sit! Stay! Bad pig!" Trey shouted.

All three Porters peered down the hall, but there was no sign of the crazed pig. "He's gone. What can

64

I say?" James told his son with a shrug. "That's why pigs aren't called 'man's best friend.' We'll check out some puppies when we get home."

Trey sank onto the bed, fighting back tears. Melanie sat down beside her brother and put her arm around him.

James saw his son's tears and shook his head. Trey was so smart, it was easy to forget he was still just a little boy.

"It's okay, son," James said at last. "I'll go find him for you."

Trey wiped his cheeks. "Thanks, Dad."

Crouched like a stalking predator, James turned a corner and checked both ends of the hall. Behind him, Melanie kept her eyes peeled. But there was no sign of Albert, not even a snout.

Melanie touched her father's shoulder. He put his fingers to his lips, urging her to be quiet. Then he gestured for Melanie to go down one hall, while he went down the other.

Following her father's silent direction, Melanie rounded the next corner and spied a cleaning woman on the floor, entangled in rolls of shredded toilet paper. Her cart lay on its side.

"*El cerdo del diablo!*" she cried.

Melanie helped the woman to her feet. "Next time we'll feed him decaf!" she promised. Then she was off, hot on Albert's trail.

James and Melanie met back up at the end of a long, dead-end corridor, where the pig watched them with wild eyes.

"We've got him cornered," Melanie whispered.

"I'll take it from here," James said. "I'm experienced in these situations."

James approached the pig in what he hoped was a totally nonthreatening manner.

"Okay, Albert. Stay calm," James said. "This doesn't have to end badly. Just come back to the room, and we'll rub your belly while you ride this OUUUUT!"

James dove for Albert. But the pig slipped from his grasp, and leaped through an open window. Kicking his stubby legs, Albert dropped down on a tent set up on the lawn below.

Melanie peered out the window and saw Albert looking through a hole in the canvas. Inside the tent sat the bride from the lobby. Standing beside her was her father.

"Looks like we've got a wedding crasher," Melanie observed.

"I'm on it!" James cried, and took off down the hall.

On the hotel's lawn, a huge sign announced: ARCARA WEDDING RECEPTION. Hundreds of guests were gathered inside the white tent, which had festively decorated tables, a dance floor, and a big buffet. The center of the tent was dominated by a huge wedding cake. As a five-piece band played, the father of the bride serenaded his blushing daughter, Lily.

When the song ended, Mr. Arcara faced the groom and raised his glass for a toast. "Ted, you'd better take care of my girl, because she is an absolute—"

"Pig!" the groom cried. He had just caught sight of Albert peering through the hole in the tent.

"Excuse me?" the bride barked—and decked her new husband with a right hook.

Rip! Everyone looked up as the tent was torn open and Albert dropped into the middle of the shrimp-cocktail platter. Red sauce splashed Lily's white gown. The crowd screamed and scattered.

"Get him!" Mr. Arcara cried, pointing to the little pig.

The ushers dived for Albert. He easily dodged them and jumped onto the buffet table, where he came face-to-face with a roast pig on a platter, an apple stuck in its mouth. A single tear rolled down the cheek of the caffeine-mad pig. Then Albert whirled and faced the wedding party, determined to avenge his baked brother!

Now the hunters became the hunted. Albert charged the guests furiously. In terror, the guests raced around the tent, the crazed pig snapping at their heels.

By now, James had entered the tent, with Melanie and Trey right behind him. They were just in time to see Albert leaping for the towering wedding cake.

Like a wide receiver, James charged through the wedding party and jumped in front of the flying pig. He made a beautiful catch worthy of a Super Bowl star.

Landing on his feet, pig in hand, he let out a shout of victory and handed the squirming pig back to Trey. That's when he noticed that the cake was teetering. James lunged to quickly steady it. He looked around at the chaos inside the tent and sighed.

"At least we saved the cake," he announced.

But it wasn't over yet. When the pandemonium ended, the exhausted groom leaned against the tent pole. With a loud crack, it broke. *Crash!* The entire tent collapsed.

"Whoops," said Trey.

CHAPTER EIGHT

"I'm sorry," the waitress said. "I know you've had a rough night, but I can only let you stay if you order something else."

James Porter was sitting at the counter of a little twenty-four–hour roadside diner. It was the only place he could find to crash with his kids after they had been thrown out of the hotel.

"I'll have another coffee, please," James told the waitress with wide-open eyes.

"You sure?" The waitress frowned. "You've already had nine cups."

"Sure, I'm sure!" James replied, completely wired.

"I feel fine. Totally fine. Finer than fine! I'm just in the mood for coffee. Uh . . . is it bad that I can hear my heartbeat?"

The waitress smiled as she refilled his mug. "You're a good dad," she whispered.

James sighed and glanced behind him at a booth. Melanie, Trey, and Albert were all sleeping in a heap. He sipped his tenth mug of coffee and checked his watch. His kids deserved some serious shut-eye, but the sun was up now, and they had to get moving.

"All right kids," he called, clapping his hands. "Time to roll!"

Melanie and Trey opened their eyes and groggily stretched.

"There's a bus station forty miles up the road," James informed them. "Let's get some food in you." He noticed Albert still snoring away on the booth seat. "Anyone up for some *pigs* in a blanket?" he asked loudly.

Albert's little piggy eyes snapped open.

Melanie pointed to the mug of coffee in her father's hand. "I thought you said coffee was a drug."

"I also said you couldn't date till you're thirty." James smirked. "You want to hold me to that, too?"

As Trey rubbed the sleep from his eyes, he began to giggle.

"What's so funny?" James asked.

Trey lowered his voice and imitated his dad. "'At least I saved the cake!'"

Melanie laughed.

James raised an eyebrow. "Oh, so you think that's funny, too?"

"It's pretty funny, Dad," said Melanie.

Trey giggled some more, and James finally cracked a smile. "They're going to have a heck of a wedding video," he admitted.

Just then, the door to the diner swung open and two familiar faces entered. It was Doug and Wendy Greenhut, the perky father-daughter duo from the Northwestern University tour.

"I don't believe it!" Wendy squealed, seeing Melanie and her family.

"What are you guys doing here?" James asked.

Doug patted his daughter's shoulder. "Me and my little cowgirl are just picking up a dozen donuts before we hit the *road-eo*. You?"

"Uh . . ." James hesitated. The real story was just too long and embarrassing, so he simply said, "We had a little bad luck with the car."

A little? Melanie thought.

"Well, new friends, your luck just changed!" Doug assured them.

But Melanie wasn't so sure. Within minutes of piling into the Greenhuts' station wagon, Doug and his daughter began singing Christmas carols. That might not have been strange if it were anywhere close to December.

Melanie shared a horrified glance with her brother. She might have shared one with her father, too, but James was actually bobbing his head in time with the out-of-season tunes.

"Don't you just love Christmas carols?" Wendy gushed between numbers. "I don't care what time of year it is; give me a chorus of 'Joy to the World,' and I'm as mad as a hatter!"

You can say that again, Melanie thought. She glanced at her dad and couldn't believe what she saw. He was giving her an "I-told-you-so" look.

"See?" he whispered. "They sing with each other. Nothing wrong with that."

Give me a break. Melanie rolled her eyes. There's a big difference between singing "Double Dutch

Bus" and visiting Santaland in springtime!

From behind the station wagon's wheel, Doug glanced over his shoulder. "So J.P.," he said to James, "you getting ready for the big day?"

"What day is that?" James asked.

"The day our precious ones shuffle off to Buffalo," Doug cheerfully replied.

"Not that I'm going to Buffalo," Wendy clarified, "though I did apply to Cornell, which is in Upstate New York."

"I'll tell you, this road trip has been such a great experience for Wendy and I," Doug said. "We've had *so much* to talk about."

"It's like we're getting to know each other all over again!" Wendy gushed.

Just then, the two glanced at each other and broke into another song—this one from an old musical.

"Key change!" Doug cried between verses.

Ten minutes later, the singing was still going strong. Melanie glanced at her father, who was still bobbing his head, but his smile was beginning to look a little plastic.

Doug and Wendy moved on to another old tune.

Trey leaned over to Melanie. "If you want," he

whispered, "Albert could poison them and make it look like an accident."

Melanie glanced at Albert. The little pig nodded and narrowed his eyes with alarming menace. Melanie shuddered. "I'll get back to you on that," she told her brother.

Another twenty minutes passed, and James Porter had given up all pretense that he was enjoying the father-daughter–palooza in the front seat. When Doug and Wendy started singing another duet, James grimaced and held his head.

Melanie stifled a laugh as she elbowed her dad in the ribs. "Yeah," she muttered, "if only we could be like them."

"Whoo!" Wendy cried when she and her dad *finally* took a singing break. She chugged a bottle of water as if it were a Broadway intermission. Then she turned in her seat. "So, Melanie, what other schools are you looking at?"

"Just one," Melanie said. "I've got a last-minute interview at Georgetown."

"Wow, Georgetown," Wendy grinned. "Great school. What would you study?"

"Prelaw," Melanie said. "I'm hoping to get

into the Cooper program."

"No way, the Cooper program!" Wendy shrieked. "I always wanted to go to Japan!"

Melanie suddenly tensed. She waved at Wendy. *Stop talking! Stop!* Melanie tried to tell her, but the girl just kept babbling!

"Japan!" James cried, finally getting a clue. "What about Japan?"

"It's the Cooper program," Wendy explained. "Melanie will get to study abroad at Georgetown's sister school. Tokyo, right?"

"Tokyo!" James was totally freaking out now.

Melanie forced a smile, but she knew she was in huge trouble with her father. For the rest of the trip, he just sat stewing. He wouldn't even glance her way. James was obviously furious to hear his daughter making plans for her future; plans that included studying halfway around the world—and she hadn't even bothered to consult him!

Fifteen minutes later, the Greenhuts' wagon finally pulled up to the bus station.

"Hey, man, I really appreciate the ride," James told Doug as the two men unloaded the Porters' luggage. James reached into his back pocket. "Can I help you out with a little gas money?"

"No, no." Doug shook his head. "But it is going to cost you—one great big hug!"

James backed up. He wasn't the hugging type. Instead, he gave Doug a pat on the shoulder. "Well, so long," James said.

Doug waved and climbed back into the car. "Farewell!" he called.

Wendy bounced up and down in her seat, waving as their car rolled away.

James shook his head, watching the father-daughter duo disappear into the distance.

A few minutes later, Melanie walked up to him. "We missed the bus," she said, pointing to the ticket window, "but I did manage to get us a lift on a tour bus."

James glared at her, still furious, then folded his arms and looked away.

Melanie sighed. "At least there won't be any singing," she muttered.

But thirty minutes later, Melanie realized she'd been wrong—about the singing, at least. As the Porters rolled down the highway with a busload of tourists, a middle-aged Japanese man stood at the front of the vehicle crooning his heart out on a karaoke machine.

James rolled his eyes. "Oh, yeah," he muttered to his daughter. "This is *much* better."

Melanie nudged her dad playfully and pointed out the window. "I spy a cow," she said with a smile. "I spy . . ."

But her game didn't work. James just scowled and continued to stew.

Melanie sighed. "Dad, I know you're angry with me but—"

James shook his head. "It's not that I'm angry. It's just . . . Look, a week ago I had no idea about Georgetown, or that you went dancing at parties, or wanted to live in Japan. You were my little girl. I feel like I don't even know you anymore."

Melanie frowned. She was ready for her dad's anger, but not this.

Just then, the man in the front of the bus finished his song. As some of the passengers applauded, Melanie made a decision. She got up from her seat, moved down the aisle, and picked up the karaoke microphone.

"Hey, everybody!" Melanie began. "I want to thank you all for giving us a ride today. I'm on a very special trip with my daddy—" She pointed him out. "And I want to do a song for him. It's one we used to sing together when I was a girl. All right, come on everyone, put your hands together!"

Melanie started clapping. A few passengers joined in. As the claps set the beat, Melanie turned to one of the tourists in the front row.

"Okay, I'm going to need you to give me a little bass." The man cleared his throat and tried. But only a squeak came out.

"You're fired." She pointed to another dude whose name tag read Mr. Matsuoka. "How about you?"

Mr. Matsuoka smiled. In a deep baritone, he began to sound out a beat.

"That's it!" Melanie cried. "Now keep it going!"

Mr. Matsuoka nodded and continued doing a righteous job on the bass part.

With her backup singers in key, Melanie dove right into the song—"Double Dutch Bus."

As she sang, Melanie grinned at her dad, but he continued to stare out the window. The man was tough! But Melanie wasn't giving up. She raised her voice and sang the refrain even louder.

Some of the passengers really started getting into it. And finally, James got into it, too. He bobbed his head in time with the beat and then he actually smiled!

Everyone jumped up and started dancing in their seats. Trey whooped as the crowd lifted him up and concert-surfed him across the bus. A moment later, Albert squealed in delight as he was lifted up and passed along as well.

Melanie laughed and danced back down the aisle to her father.

"And you said you didn't remember," James teased.

"Of course I remember!" Melanie assured him. Then she sat down next to her big papa bear and put her head on his shoulder.

The bus zoomed toward the horizon, and father and daughter both smiled, listening to the whole bus sing their song.

CHAPTER NINE

"Now just make a left down Maple," James told the bus driver as he turned down a dark, treelined street. "Three blocks and we're there. . . . "

Melanie tugged her dad's sleeve. "Does Grandma know we're still coming?"

"I didn't call her, but it's not like she's going anywhere," James said. "Just remember, she's an old woman now. She's not as light on her feet."

"Wheee!" Grandma Porter cried, kicking up her heels.

At that very moment, she and her boyfriend, Harold, were having a salsa dancing party in her living room. Two other elderly couples were strutting and dipping right along with them. All of them were decked out in colorful Latin costumes.

As Harold spun her around, Grandma Porter noticed bright headlights coming down her street. She peered out the window and saw a big tour bus pulling up to the curb. The bus door opened, and she saw James climbing down the steps.

"It's my son!" she shouted.

"The control freak?" asked one of the gray-haired women.

"We're busted!" Harold shouted.

"Hide!" Grandma ordered.

While everyone scrambled to find a hiding place, Grandma turned off the music.

Meanwhile, just outside, the big tour bus pulled away from the curb. Mr. Matsuoka waved to James and his kids.

James waved and glanced down at his daughter. "You've created a monster."

Then James laughed. So did Melanie. Arm and arm, they walked up the steps.

"Here we are," James announced. "Home sweet home. I just hope the surprise isn't too much of a shock for my mama's fragile heart."

He knocked on the front door.

"One second!" Grandma shouted.

Finally, the door opened. "We're here!" James, Melanie, and Trey called out in unison.

"Oh, my goodness!" said Grandma Porter. By now, she'd changed clothes and looked like a typical, sweet old lady with a baggy dress and sensible shoes. Only one thing didn't go with the outfit—the giant gardenia she'd been wearing in her hair as part of her colorful salsa costume.

Melanie didn't notice the gardenia. She was too busy rushing toward her grandmother to give her a big hug.

"Not so rough, you'll break her!" James warned. Then he stepped up himself to give the old woman a *gentle* hug. "Good to see you, Mama. What's in your hair?"

Grandma's eyes widened, and she realized she'd forgotten about her salsa costume's gardenia. "Oh!" she said, reaching up to pluck it out. "What is that? I must've been in the garden. Good to see you!"

Just then, Harold stepped out onto the porch. Still wearing his loud salsa clothes, he smiled down at Grandma. "I watered the lilies in the kitchen, Mrs. Porter," he said with a sly wink.

Grandma gulped. "Uh, thank you, Harold." She turned to her son. "James, this is Harold, my, uh . . . gardener."

The two men shook hands. Then James pointed to the front yard. "You might want to get on those hedges."

Harold stiffened. "Next time," he said, brushing by James to leave.

Grandma waved her family inside and closed the door. As James walked through the house, Grandma's dancing buddies snuck out the windows.

"So, how's that new security system working out?" James asked. "Do you like it?"

"Yes, it's fine." Grandma nodded. "I finally feel protected from *all* the crime here in *rural* Pennsylvania."

"Just *fine*?" James said. "Melanie, check this out." He punched a keypad on the wall. Then he quickly slipped on his sunglasses and opened the front door. "Motion sensors and . . ." He tossed a piece of paper into the yard, and, suddenly, massive floodlights came on, making the nighttime shine like noon.

"Ahh!" Melanie, Grandma, and Trey were all blinded.

"Floodlights!" James cried before deactivating the system again. "Pretty impressive, right?"

As Melanie tried to rub the spots from her eyes, she heard a familiar combination of sounds—a honking car horn and the blare of girly music.

"I don't believe it!" Melanie cried.

James froze. He knew those sounds, too.

Sure enough, when Melanie ran to the window, she saw Katie and Nancy climbing out of Katie's car. Melanie screamed as her friends came to the front door. Then all three girls started jumping up and down, squealing in delight.

James sighed, watching the scene with growing concern.

"What are you guys doing here?" Melanie asked.

"Yeah." James frowned and folded his arms. "What are you guys doing here?"

Katie grinned at Melanie. "After you couldn't make it yesterday, we decided to stay at my sister's an extra night and surprise you."

"Your mom told us where you'd be," Nancy said.

Katie's head bobbed excitedly. "Now you can come sleep over at my sister's just like we planned it!"

"Ohmigosh!" Melanie cried. "That's okay with you, Dad, right? You said you were totally cool with it, remember?"

James stared at his daughter. He knew he had no choice. "Oh, yeah," he mumbled. "Totally. Like I said . . ."

"I can't believe this!" Melanie squealed. "Can you believe it? Isn't this the best?"

"The *best-est*," James grumbled. Then he brightened with a thought. "But your *grandma* hasn't had much time with you." He turned, expecting parental backup from his sweet, old mama.

"Go!" Grandma told her granddaughter. "Have a good time!"

James gritted his teeth as Melanie kissed them both good-bye.

"Good night, guys!" she sang. "See you tomorrow!"

"Remember," James sternly called after her, "we have a ten o'clock flight to D.C. in the morning."

Melanie nodded. "I'll be back by eight!"

James watched his daughter depart. Reluctantly,

he closed the door and returned to his mother's living room. There was nothing he could to now.

"Good night, James," Grandma Porter said.

As James kissed his mother good night, Trey wandered in and plopped down on the sofa. "Albert and I are going to sleep, too," he announced.

"Okay," James said. "Good night, son."

"I just want you to know I think it's cool that you're letting Melanie spend the night with her friends."

"Yeah, well . . ." James shrugged. "I was pretty much boxed into a corner on that one."

Trey chewed his lower lip. "You still mad at me for coming on the trip?"

James folded his arms and smiled. "Come on, son. I could never stay mad at you. You're my little man."

Trey exhaled in relief. "I love you, Dad."

"I love you, too." James kissed his son good night, and Trey headed off for bed, Albert trotting behind.

James glanced around the room. He was all alone and not a bit sleepy, so he plopped down on an easy chair, grabbed the TV remote, and began flipping through channels.

On one channel, he noticed the opening credits for an animal show. James leaned back against the chair cushions, contented at last.

"The baby gazelle remains at its father's side," the TV announcer explained, "seeking protection and security."

James smiled. This sounded promising.

Then his smile vanished. "For if it veers off," the announcer went on, "it becomes vulnerable to a myriad of vicious predators."

"What are you doing, gazelle?" James barked at the TV. "Stay with your daddy. Run. Run!"

On the screen, the baby gazelle couldn't hear James's fatherly warning. Too late, it was caught by a hungry lion. "Without the parent's guidance," the announcer droned, "the offspring are at the mercy of the harsh and unforgiving world. . . ."

James covered his eyes, unable to watch anymore. He stood up and began to pace. Finally, he picked up his cell phone and dialed Melanie's number.

At the sorority house, Melanie walked out of her assigned bedroom and headed into the restroom. A moment later, back in her room, her cell phone rang.

One of the sorority girls heard the phone ringing. Chris was just getting over a terrible cold, so when she spoke, her deep, gravelly voice made her sound like a gruff man.

"Hello?" Chris said, answering Melanie's phone.

"Who is this?" James demanded on the other end.

"It's Chris."

"Chris?" James barked. "What are you doing there?"

"I live here," Chris replied.

"Where's Melanie?" James demanded.

Chris scratched her head. "I think she's in the shower," her deep, manly voice replied. Just then, Chris noticed another girl in the hall.

"Hey, Bobby," Chris's deep voice called. "Go see if Melanie's in the shower."

"Bobby!" James repeated in horror.

A second later, Melanie's dad was hanging up and running for the front door. He flung it open and raced out into the night, forgetting all about his fancy security alarm's floodlights. The burning bulbs kicked on, and James was instantly blinded.

"Ow! Whoa!" he cried, before tripping all the way down his mother's front steps.

CHAPTER TEN

James drove like a madman to the University of Pittsburgh. He pulled up to the sorority house where his daughter was staying and jogged up to the entrance. But the door was locked! He pulled once more, but it just wouldn't budge. In frustration, he began pounding on it.

Finally, the housemother appeared—and she didn't look happy. "Can I help you?" she asked, sticking her head out the door.

"I need to see my daughter," James announced.

The housemother nodded. "Who's your daughter?"

"Melanie Porter," James said. Then he hit his forehead. "Oh, she's not a student here. She's spending the night. It'll just take a minute—" James tried to step around the woman, but the housemother jammed her hand into his chest.

"Who's she staying with?" the woman demanded.

"Katie's sister," James replied.

The housemother folded her big arms. "Katie's sister." She raised an eyebrow. "You're going to have to do better than that."

"It's okay." James tossed her a superior smile. "I'm a police officer."

"Great. Your badge, Officer?" The housemother held out her hand.

James nodded. "Good for you. Good security sense." He patted his pockets, and then he realized. *Not again!*

"See, I just ran out," he told the woman. "I left my badge back at my mom's."

The housemother narrowed her eyes. "You still live with your mother?"

James shook his head and almost laughed. "I know what this sounds like. . . ."

"Sounds like you're not getting in my sorority!"

Before James could say another word, the house-mother slammed the door shut and threw the dead bolt. In frustration, James marched back to the curb. He looked up to the second floor, scanning the lighted windows. Finally, he saw his daughter. Melanie's arms were flailing. It looked like she was in trouble!

"Melanie! Melanie!" He shouted, but she couldn't hear him.

That's when James noticed some painting equipment stored against a nearby building. He grabbed the collapsible ladder, leaned it against the sorority house, and climbed to the second floor.

When he got to Melanie's bedroom window, he finally saw what was really happening. She wasn't in trouble. She was just dancing with her girlfriends. She hadn't heard him calling because the music was so loud.

He watched for a few minutes—there were no boys in sight. With a smile of relief, James realized he had overreacted. He was about to climb back down the ladder and leave when—*Shink-shink-shink-shink!* James's eyes bugged as the ladder collapsed right out from under him!

In desperation, he hung on to the second floor windowsill.

Inside, Melanie and her friends were still dancing to the music. Then someone shouted from the hallway, and they all ran out of the room.

Hanging on for dear life, James opened the window and pulled himself through. *Thud!* He fell to the floor. Shaking his head, he looked around. There were a number of beds, some dressers and closets, and the walls were plastered with posters of Hollywood stars.

I've got to get out of here! James thought. He scrambled to his feet and tiptoed to the hallway. He was ready to sneak out when he saw Melanie and her two best friends heading his way.

James shut the door and tried not to panic. He couldn't go back out through the window—not without a trip to the hospital. He was going to have to hide! As the girls' voices got closer, James dived under one of the beds.

Melanie and her friends came back into the room, chatting up a storm. They turned the music up and started dancing again. In a fit of excitement, the girls jumped onto one of the beds.

James squeezed his eyes shut as the bedsprings above him smashed against his back.

". . . so I get up and sing, 'Double Dutch Bus' and the whole bus turns into a party!" Melanie said, laughing.

"What's 'Double Dutch Bus'?" Katie asked.

"It's this song me and my dad used to sing when I was a kid," Melanie explained. "It's kind of our song."

"I totally have a song with my dad," said Katie's older sister, Ally.

Ally reached over and put another CD in the player. "You're the Inspiration" by the band Chicago began to play.

"Put it on repeat, Ally," Katie told her sister.

James sighed and checked his digital watch: 10:32. That seemed pretty late to him. He figured the girls would listen to the song a few times and just doze off. Then he could sneak back out. Problem solved.

But the girls didn't doze off.

At 12:08, James could still hear them talking. The *same* song continued to play while underneath the bed, James unconsciously mouthed the lyrics. By now, they had burned themselves into his brain.

"So, Mel," Katie said. "Looks like you and Hunter may actually end up at the same college."

"Looks that way," Melanie replied.

Beneath the bed, James scowled. *Hunter?*

Katie laughed. "Your dad would have an aneurysm if he knew!"

"Actually, things are really pretty good between us," Melanie said. "I mean, my dad was totally cool about my coming here, which I know wasn't easy for him. I think maybe he's really starting to trust me. Respect me even."

"Awwwwww," the girls replied together.

Under the bed, James sighed, feeling very guilty.

By 1:24, the room had gone completely quiet—except for that same song, which started from the beginning again. By now James was tearing his hair out. Singing along to the tune was no longer an option. He just wanted it to stop!

On the bright side, the girls finally seemed to be asleep. With a deep breath, James carefully moved his body out from under the low-hanging mattress. But just as he was about to rise and head for the door, Katie asked—

"Mel? Do you think I should get my hair straightened?"

James struck his own forehead—several times.

"It could look really pretty," Melanie said on a yawn. "What do you think, Nancy? Nancy?"

"She's asleep." Melanie giggled. "What celebrity does Nancy look like when she sleeps? I'll give you fifty guesses."

James froze. *Fifty* guesses? He checked his watch again and shuddered.

Forty-five minutes later, the girls *seemed* to be fast asleep. James got ready to make a break for it again, when—

"What do you make of that whole situation in Darfur anyway?" Katie asked.

Beneath the bed, James whimpered like a sad puppy.

At 4:32, "You're the Inspiration" came to an end—again. *Silence.* Like a prisoner of war subjected to brutal torture tactics, James was starting to break. His lips were quivering and his eye was twitching. "Please no. Please not again," he murmured, but the song started up once more. "Make it stop, make it stop . . ."

Early the next morning, Melanie waved to her friends as they pulled away from her grandma's house. She walked inside to find Trey munching on cornflakes.

"Where's Dad?" Melanie asked.

Trey shrugged. Grandma Porter didn't know where James was either. Perplexed, Melanie pulled out her cell phone and called her dad.

"No answer," she said. "Where is he? We're going to miss our flight."

Trey shrugged again, continuing to munch. Then Melanie's phone rang. She quickly answered.

"Hello? . . . This is she . . . What? . . . He's *where?*"

"For the last time," James told the campus security guard, "I'm a chief of police back in Illinois. My badge is at my mom's house. I just snuck into the sorority because I thought my daughter was in danger."

The guard snorted. "I've heard that one before."

Just then, Melanie arrived at the campus security office. She didn't see anyone at the front desk, so she rang the bell—several times. Finally, the guard who'd been talking to her father walked out of another room, closing the door behind him.

"I'm Melanie Porter," she told the big man. "Somebody just called about my dad. Is he okay?"

The security guard nodded. "The individual in custody was discovered on campus this morning sleeping under a girl's bed at one of the sorority houses."

"Can I see him?" Melanie asked.

The guard walked back to the room he'd just left and opened the door. Melanie's jaw dropped. Her father was sitting on a metal folding chair with his wrist handcuffed to the leg of a heavy table.

"Baby girl!" James cried. "You're not going to believe what happened. See, I tried calling you, but this guy answered. I mean, I thought it was a guy, and . . . isn't that funny?"

Wounded, Melanie just stared. Then she turned to the guard and said, "That man's not my father."

"Melanie Eloise Porter!" James cried in shock.

"Because *my* father would never cross the line like that," Melanie snapped. "*My* father would trust me to make smart choices."

James smirked. "Like the smart choice of picking your college based on a guy?"

Melanie blinked. "What are you talking about?"

"You can drop the whole foreign-study bit," James said. "I know what program really interests you at Georgetown—the *Hunter* program."

"What?" Melanie asked.

James folded his arms. "I heard you talking with your girlfriends last night, Melanie."

Melanie put a hand on her hip. "Actually, what you heard was that Hunter and I might end up going to college together at *Northwestern*."

"Wait, you mean, Hunter—"

"—is going to Northwestern," Melanie snapped. "I can't believe you think I would plan my whole future around some cute boy!"

Melanie turned to the guard. "Like I said, this man couldn't be my father. He obviously doesn't know me. Now if you'll excuse me, I'm very late for a flight."

As she headed for the door, her dad rose to his feet. "Melanie," James barked. "Don't you walk away from me. Melanie!"

But it was too late. Melanie was gone.

CHAPTER ELEVEN

"You're free to go," the guard told James a short time later. He unlocked his handcuffs. "Someone sprung you."

James rose quickly. With hope in his heart, he strode out of the holding room, looking for his daughter. But the only person waiting for him was Grandma Porter, sitting on a wooden bench near the door.

"Mama?" James said. "What's going on? Where's Melanie and Trey?"

"Trey's taking Albert for a walk, and Melanie is

trying to catch her plane," Grandma replied.

James exploded. "You let her go without me?"

Grandma sighed and patted the bench beside her. "Sit down, James."

James frowned. His mother was using a tone he hadn't heard since he'd been a teenager. Automatically cowed, he sat down on the bench.

"Melanie told me what happened at Northwestern," his mama said.

"I can explain—" James began, but Grandma Porter cut him off.

"You didn't want her to go to Georgetown so you concocted some ridiculous plan—"

"It wasn't ridiculous!" James cried.

"A fake student, James?"

James frowned, momentarily speechless.

"I have something to tell you," Grandma finally admitted.

"What?" James asked.

"Harold is not my gardener. He's my boyfriend."

"Whoa!" James leaped up from his seat. "What?"

Grandma shrugged. "I met him when I was taking salsa-dancing classes."

"You don't dance!"

"I most certainly do," Grandma sniffed proudly. "And I'm good."

"Wait. What does this have to do with—"

Grandma pointed to the bench again. With a groan, James sat back down.

"For years now, I've had to pretend I was someone else just to make you feel better," Grandma confessed. "I knew if I told you that I was staying out late salsa dancing with my boyfriend, you would never stop worrying about me. So I just didn't tell you."

James rubbed a hand over his face. "And what does this have to do with Melanie?"

Grandma shook her head. "James, my beautiful boy . . . you are a control freak."

"No, I'm not!"

"You performed a sting operation on your own daughter just to get her to go to Northwestern," Grandma pointed out. "You turned my home into a high-security prison. You can't even let Melanie spend the night with some friends without creeping around like a cat burglar."

"What do you expect me to do?" James threw up his hands. "How am I supposed to know she's safe if she goes all the way to Washington!"

Grandma shook her finger. "As a young man *you* decided to join the Air Force. What do you think that was like for me? I wanted you to come home every day that you were gone, but I had to trust you. I had to trust that you could take care of yourself. I had to believe in you. Why can't you believe in her?"

James shook his head. "It's my baby, Mama," he whispered.

"Son, your *baby* is a young *woman*—smart, beautiful, capable, and ready to take on the world. Any fool can see it. Why can't you?"

James was quiet a long moment. Then he met his mother's eyes. "Mama, you've got to get me to the airport. I've got to make this right."

"Now you're talking." Grandma smiled and slapped her son's leg. "Let's roll!"

As Grandma pulled her car up to the airport, James turned to face the backseat. "I'll see you two back home," he told Trey and Albert.

Trey nodded. "Is Mom going to kill me?"

James raised an eyebrow. "I got your back on this one, son. Just don't let it happen again."

Trey lifted a fist. "Good luck."

James smiled and knocked knuckles with his son. "Thanks."

"You'll need this," Grandma said before James left the car. She handed him his badge.

James kissed his mama's cheek. Then he raced into the airport. He *had* to get to Melanie before her plane departed! He ran to the gate, but the door to the boarding ramp was already closed.

"The flight to D.C.," he said to an employee behind the desk. "Has it left yet?"

"About twenty minutes ago, sir," the woman told him.

James's shoulders sagged. Feeling totally defeated, he turned from the desk—and saw his daughter! Melanie was sitting alone in the waiting area.

James walked up to her. "Melanie . . ."

Melanie looked up. Her eyes were red from crying.

At the sight of her tears, James felt his heart sink. "You missed the flight." He shook his head. "This is all my fault. I'm sorry."

"It's okay." Melanie wiped her eyes. "I guess it just wasn't meant to be."

James sat down next to his daughter. "Look, a lot of bad stuff's happened on this trip. And some of it has been caused by me—"

Melanie gave him a look.

"Okay," James said, "*most* of it was caused by me. But maybe I needed to go through all this to realize that my baby girl isn't a baby anymore. You're a young woman, and you've got your own worlds to conquer. So, whatever makes my daughter happy, that's what it's all about now."

Melanie blinked, astonished to hear those words coming from her control-freak father. But he *had* said the words. And Melanie was very glad. She opened her arms, and they hugged.

James was thrilled that his daughter forgave him. But he *still* needed to make things right! That's when he noticed a small plane outside the window. The words WASHINGTON, D.C., were painted on its side.

With a *whoop*, he turned to his daughter. "Come on!"

Before Melanie knew what was happening, her dad grabbed her hand and pulled her out onto the airport tarmac.

"You trust me, right?" he called to her as they ran toward the plane.

Melanie nodded. "Of course."

When they reached the small plane, a handful of people were boarding it. Strangely, they were all wearing red jumpsuits. James called out to one man, and quickly introduced himself. The young man said his name was Donny.

"You guys going to Washington?" James asked.

"Yeah," Donny replied, "but the plane is for team members only."

That explained the matching suits, Melanie thought.

James pulled out his badge. "We've got a police emergency. You *have* to let us on that plane!"

Donny stared at the badge and scratched his head. "Are you guys divers?"

"Oh, yeah. Big time," James nodded, glancing at his daughter. "Huge divers." He *had* been swimming before. That had to count, right?

Melanie's head bobbed. "Since I was a little girl."

Donny smiled. "Then climb aboard!"

James and Melanie boarded the plane and took seats on one of the two long benches. Weird, Melanie thought. Why don't they have regular seats?

The plane soared through the air, and James glanced out the window. He smiled at Melanie, pleased with himself for finding a way to D.C.

"I've never heard of a diving team having its own plane," James remarked to Donny.

Donny nodded. "Most do."

"Really?" James said.

Donny laughed. "It's pretty hard to do our thing without one."

James shrugged. "I thought all you needed was a swimming pool and a bouncy board."

The other team members glanced at each other. Some of them were chuckling. James's remark seemed to amuse them.

"Wrong kind of diving team, man," Donny told the police chief.

"Well, what sort of diving team are you?" James asked.

Just then someone opened up a door in the plane's side. Melanie's eyes widened. "Dad, they're a *sky*diving team!" she cried.

James froze. "Wait a minute, you're not *landing* in D.C.?"

"*We* are," Donny replied. "The plane's not."

"But we need to get to Georgetown right now!" James exclaimed.

"There's only one way that's going to happen," Donny said and tossed James a parachute.

"Ahhhhhh!" Melanie cried.

Father and daughter hadn't even jumped yet. They simply stood at the plane's open door, wearing helmets and red jumpsuits, staring at the ground far below. *Really* far below!

"Okay," Donny warned them sternly. "We've been doing this for six minutes now. We're making *one* more circle, and then the plane's turning around."

All of the other skydivers had jumped. Melanie looked at her watch. "Time's running out," she told her dad.

"We can do this," James assured Melanie. "I've done it a million times before."

Melanie stared. "You never told me you jumped out of a plane."

"We'll talk about it later," James said. He'd sky-dived in the Air Force. It was a long time ago, but James told himself it would all come back to him. It was like riding a bike. "Right now, we have an appointment to make," he reminded Melanie. "Okay. On three. One, two, three!"

Melanie closed her eyes and together she and her father finally jumped.

Donny grinned and put on his goggles. "Now that's one cool dad!" he said before jumping himself.

Melanie and James soared through the blue sky. Donny had rigged them to jump in tandem, so they were attached to each other, sharing one parachute. Both were screaming their heads off, arms flailing.

"Dad! Pull the cord!" Melanie shouted.

"What?" James's eyes were wide. Clearly, he'd forgotten pretty much *everything* about riding *this* bike!

"Pull the cord!" Melanie reminded him.

Oh, yeah! James pulled the cord. *Phmmph!* Their parachute opened, suddenly jerking them up. And then they started floating down.

"We did it!" Melanie shrieked with joy.

"Yeah!" James grinned. Then his face fell. "Little problem."

"What?" Mel asked.

"This isn't a parachute," James realized. "It's a *parasail!*"

The big wing wasn't taking them straight down with the other skydivers. It was sailing them in another direction altogether.

"Ahhhhhhhhh!" cried Melanie and James.

Suddenly, James realized where they were landing. "Look! There's a golf course right below us. We'll be safe there!"

CHAPTER TWELVE

"Fore!" James shouted.

Below him a golfer was about to putt his final hole. The man heard the shout of warning but couldn't figure out where it was coming from. Too late, he looked up—

Wham!

James and Melanie landed right on him! All three rolled off the green and into a duck pond. James and Melanie became unattached as they rolled to a stop. Laughing, Melanie slogged out of the water. She couldn't believe it—they had actually made it!

Together, she and her dad went to help the golfer they'd knocked down. James grabbed a sand-trap rake and held it out to the man, who was flailing his arms and sputtering.

"Sorry about that," James called. "Are you okay?"

"I'm—" The man stopped sputtering. With the horror of recognition, he looked straight into James's face. *"You!"*

Uh-oh. Melanie finally recognized the dude. It was Mr. Arcara, the father of the bride from the wedding Albert had totally ruined.

"Oh, boy," Melanie whispered.

"Listen," James told the man. "There's a really good explanation for this. You see, I'm trying to get my daughter to her college interview and—"

"I'll kill you!" Mr. Arcara shouted.

"Maybe some other time," James said as he let go of the rake.

Splash! Mr. Arcara fell back into the pond!

James and Melanie raced to the man's golf cart and climbed in.

Sputtering, Mr. Arcara crawled out of the water. "That's my cart!" he yelled.

"We'll have it back soon," James called over his

shoulder as they sped off.

Mr. Arcara ran to his friend's golf cart. "Don't just stand there, Rocco. Let's get them!" Rocco jumped behind the wheel and they sped off.

James drove the little cart as fast as it would go. "We've got ten minutes to spare," he told Melanie. In the distance, they could see the Georgetown campus. "Ain't no stopping us now!" James said.

Bam!

The golf cart was rammed from behind.

"Dad!" Melanie cried.

James peered over his shoulder. Mr. Arcara and Rocco were following in a second cart. And they were about to ram them again!

Bam! Bam!

James fought for control of his vehicle. "What are you doing?" he shouted

"Pay back!" Mr. Arcara yelled, shaking his fist.

"*Ohmigosh!*" Melanie shrieked. They obviously weren't joking. Well, neither was she! In the back of the cart, she found a bag of golf balls. As they left the course and entered the Georgetown campus, Melanie started whipping them at Mr. Arcara and

Rocco as fast as she could.

Bop! Bop! Bop!

The golf balls bounced off their bodies. Enraged by the pummeling, Mr. Arcara pulled out a golf club and brandished it like a weapon.

"Are you out of your mind?" James yelled.

The carts were now side by side. Mr. Arcara swung the club at James. He missed, but succeeded in making the chief very angry.

"Melanie, hand me the four iron and take the wheel!" James commanded

With Melanie steering, James took a swing right back at Mr. Arcara. Suddenly, the two men were dueling—only they were using golf clubs instead of swords.

Melanie steered them around a sharp corner. Ahead of them, on the college green, she spied a huge banner for the annual Georgetown Greek Week Games. Under the sign, hundreds of students were gathered for a party, most of them wearing togas!

Melanie swerved to avoid running them over. James ducked a swing.

"How are we lookin'?" he asked.

"Lookin' good," Melanie replied. Then her eyes grew wide when she saw a drop-off right in front of them.

"Not lookin' good," she warned.

Both carts soared over the edge of the hill. They landed at the bottom with a slam that nearly threw James out of his seat.

The carts continued forward, toward the Georgetown marching band. The bandleader spied the speeding vehicles and yelled. Band members screamed as the carts scattered them.

"Looking forward to meeting you at orientation!" Melanie shouted. Then she glanced over her shoulder.

"Dad," she cried. "He's still following us!"

James took the wheel again. "Time for him to go," he announced. "You still trust me, right?"

Melanie nodded. "Always."

James swerved the cart, aiming for a low stage that had been set up beside a deep pond. Melanie saw the looming platform and freaked.

"Dad!" she cried.

"Hold on, Mel," her father commanded. "I'm not one of Illinois's finest for nothing!"

The stage was all Melanie could see.

"Duck on my count," James told her. "One, two, three, *duck*!"

Father and daughter ducked as the golf cart sped under the stage, tearing away the golf cart's canvas roof. A split-second later, the cart emerged from the other side, and James and Melanie sat up again.

The golf cart behind them didn't fare so well. Panicked, Rocco swerved to avoid colliding with the stage. *Splash!* He rolled them right into the pond.

Sputtering, Mr. Arcara bobbed to the surface in time to see Melanie waving good-bye as the other golf cart turned a corner.

Two minutes later, James braked their cart in front of the undergraduate-admissions building. They raced up the stairs. As they reached the front doors, Melanie glanced at the giant clock above them. It read 3:59.

"We've got a minute to go!" James cried.

They dashed inside.

"Fourth floor!" Mel told her father.

They rushed to the elevator. James pushed the button—one, two, *three* times! The doors finally opened. But the elevator car was completely packed with students wearing togas!

"Not going to work," James told his daughter.

"Come on!" Melanie raced for the stairs.

The two ran up one flight, then another, and *another*. Panting and desperate, Melanie and James finally burst through the fourth-floor door.

They flailed around as James helped Melanie out of her skydiving jumpsuit. James took the helmet from her head, and his eyes bugged. Her hair was now sculpted in the *shape* of the helmet!

"How do I look?" Melanie asked, trying to smooth the wrinkles from her outfit.

James smiled and touched her cheek. "Like an angel."

Melanie grinned and dashed to the front desk. "Hi . . ." she told the receptionist, still panting slightly from the steps. "Melanie Porter. I have an appointment with the admissions committee."

"Of course," said the receptionist, pausing a moment to take in Melanie's breathless, wrinkled, helmet-head appearance. "Welcome to Georgetown, Ms. Porter," she said sincerely. "They're all waiting for you inside. Best of luck!"

The receptionist gestured to the door behind her.

Finally the moment had come. Just one more door. After all she'd been through, just a few more steps, and she'd be home free. Melanie took a deep breath, and—

She couldn't move. She just stood there, frozen in place.

James rushed up to her. "Are you going in?"

"I can't," she whispered. "I can't do it." She met her father's eyes. "Dad, I'm afraid."

"Well, guess what? I was afraid, too."

"You?" Melanie said. "What were you afraid of?" The skydiving, she guessed. The Pitt security guards? The crazy fisherman with the hook?

James looked into his daughter's eyes. "I was afraid that if I let you go, you'd never need your daddy again."

Melanie's eyes filled with tears. "But I'm always going to need you."

"Mel, listen to me. This is what you've *got* to do now. You've got to walk in there with confidence, with your head up. Do your best, and all you can do is win."

Melanie took a deep breath and smiled. "I like that."

"If they don't accept you after that, then it's *their* loss."

Melanie hugged her father. "I'm so glad you're my dad."

"Time for you to shine," James told her. Then he kissed her forehead. "Come on, baby. Let's go. . . ."

EPILOGUE

Five months later...

"Let's go, Melanie!" James called.

Decked out in full Georgetown gear, James was just about finished unloading his repaired SUV. There was only one trunk left to go.

Melanie ran up and grabbed the other end of her trunk. She and James carried it to the registration desk, where volunteers with luggage carts were waiting to help.

Nearby, Melanie's family was gathered. Her mom,

little brother, grandmother, and a fully grown Albert had come to wish her well as she started her freshman year.

Melanie stopped at her dormitory's sign-in table. "Melanie Porter," she proudly told the resident assistant.

"Porter? Here we go." The woman handed Melanie the key to her very first dorm room. "You're in 217."

"Ahhhhhh!" cried a familiar voice.

Melanie turned to see Wendy Greenhut holding up her own dorm-room key. "I don't believe it!" shrieked the girl. "Can you believe it?! I'm in room 218!"

Melanie's eyes widened. "No!"

Wendy raced up to Melanie and gave her a big hug.

"You inspired me to apply here, and now we're neighbors!" Wendy grinned. "You and I are going to be best friends; we're going to have so much fun. I have to get my dad. He'll be so excited to see you!"

As Wendy ran off to find her father, Melanie turned to face her mom and dad. "Well . . ." she said with a deep, excited breath. "Guess this is it."

Michelle smiled. "Come here, baby."

Melanie hugged her mom and then turned to her dad. The man looked ready to cry.

"I never thought this day would come," Melanie told her father.

"I did," James said with a heavy sigh. "But I am proud of you."

Melanie opened her arms. "I love you, Daddy."

"I love you, too," he whispered, hugging her tight. "See you at Thanksgiving." Then, at long last, James Porter let his daughter go.

Melanie waved good-bye to her family and turned to face her brand new life.

I'll miss them, she told herself, but I'll see them again soon. Then she squared her shoulders and strode into her Georgetown dorm. Now that her college dream had come true, she knew it was time to start making the *rest* of her dreams a reality.

Michelle put her arm around her husband. "You going to be okay?"

James sniffed. "Where did the time go?"

"Come on, baby," she told her big, brave police chief hero. "Let's head home."

Trey tugged on his dad's jacket. "Georgetown's really great, Dad."

James looked down at his son and shook his head. No way, he thought. Not another one! "You think Georgetown's great?" he said, resting a hand on his boy's shoulder. "Have I ever told you about the animal studies program at *Northwestern*?"

Michelle rolled her eyes. "Here we go again."

"Hey, Albert, did you hear that?" Trey looked around, but his pet pig had disappeared. "Albert? Where'd you go?"

Just then, the Porters heard the sound of people screaming. An energy drink promotional tent had been set up on the campus lawn. Students were leaping out of the big, white, caffeine-happy tent.

James, Michelle, and Trey stared in horror. "Albert!"

Always the hero, James raced for the tent and leaped into it.

Crash! The tent collapsed.

"Whoops," Trey murmured in disbelief. "They did it again."

When Mrs. Porter finally arrived back home with

her husband and son, things began to get back to normal. Her oldest child was settled in college. Her husband was back on his job at the police station, and her bright little boy was back in his bedroom working on yet another one of his experiments with the help of his pig.

With everything so quiet, she was surprised to see a big, black limousine pull up to her house. The vehicle had an official U.S. government seal on the door. It swung open and out walked an Army general. He strode right up to her front door flanked by several military policemen.

"Can I . . . help you?" Michelle asked the man.

"Mrs. Porter, I must speak with your son."

Trey and Albert both came to the door. When Trey saw the general, his face lit up.

"Trey," the general said, "a situation has come up that's a matter of national security." He turned to Mrs. Porter. "Ma'am, your country needs your son . . . and his pig."

Outside, the limo door opened again and the Joint Chiefs of Staff started walking toward the Porters' front door. Mrs. Porter's jaw dropped. She grabbed her cell phone and speed-dialed her husband.

Trey tugged on his mom's sleeve. "I tried to tell you."

"James, it's me," Mrs. Porter whispered into her cell. "You are not going to believe this. . . ."